Anna Gallo's Lily

Anna Gallo's Lily

SUE MORRIS

Copyright © 2024 Sue Morris

The moral right of the author has been asserted.

Apart from any fair dealing for the purposes of research or private study, or criticism or review, as permitted under the Copyright, Designs and Patents Act 1988, this publication may only be reproduced, stored or transmitted, in any form or by any means, with the prior permission in writing of the publishers, or in the case of reprographic reproduction in accordance with the terms of licences issued by the Copyright Licensing Agency. Enquiries concerning reproduction outside those terms should be sent to the publishers.

This is a work of fiction. Names, characters, businesses, places, events and incidents are either the products of the author's imagination or used in a fictitious manner. Any resemblance to actual persons, living or dead, or actual events is purely coincidental.

Troubador Publishing Ltd
Unit E2 Airfield Business Park,
Harrison Road, Market Harborough,
Leicestershire LE16 7UL
Tel: 0116 279 2299
Email: books@troubador.co.uk
Web: www.troubador.co.uk

ISBN 978-1-80514-470-0

British Library Cataloguing in Publication Data.
A catalogue record for this book is available from the British Library.

Printed by Printed and bound by CPI Group (UK) Ltd, Croydon, CR0 4YY
Typeset in 11pt Minion by Troubador Publishing Ltd, Leicester, UK

To my son, Marley
And for my late father, Lawrence

AUTHOR'S NOTE

It has been more than ten years since I first formed the ideas behind *Anna Gallo's Lily* and it is only now that I have felt able to truly bring those initial thoughts to life. This debut novella, whilst fictitious, pays homage to the people and characters I have known well and those I merely observed from a distance; snippets of many lives that merge and mesh. Alongside the much needed research I undertook, the writing of the story became seamless and one of absolute joy. I hope, as I am, that you too are filled with wonder, the possibility of coincidence, and the importance of family ties. And, of course, spiced with the odd surprise and twist.

Chapter 1

The re-opening of Lily bed and breakfast, April 1965

The first guest had not meant to find herself there at all – she was misplaced, having found herself lost, driving north and not her intended east. So when she arrived at 11 a.m., there was nothing to do, apart from find somewhere to lay down her confusion. Finding no front doorbell, she walked slowly around the cottage, intermittently peering through the Windowlene of the windows, until she heard the front door open hesitantly and came face to face with a woman. Deciphering her age was nigh impossible. She seemed both young and old. She walked with a slight stutter, but when she spoke, her voice had the nuance of youth, polite in its childness.

The woman, Teresa observed, was a difficult woman to read. There was a familiarity about her. She was clothed in textures and colours that didn't give much away. Around her shoulders, she wore a heavy patchwork shawl-cum-poncho and her baggy slacks were stained green at both knees. Her feet were clad in heavy gardener's boots. Her woollen hat all but covered up whatever hair she had. It must be brought to call that the woman showed all the signs of hardship.

The woman enquired as to what she wanted and the reason for the late-morning knock at the door. Teresa explained her predicament, to which the woman answered with a simple, well you had better come in then – neither friendly nor unfriendly, just with a tone of polite indifference.

We don't actually open until Friday, noting that the day was only Monday. The rooms aren't quite ready – the kitchen cupboards need filling and the bathroom is still wet with paint, and the curtains need hanging, the floors need scrubbing and the Aga cleaning …

Sensing the woman's consternation, Teresa asked if it was okay to stay just one night, and then she would set off directly in the morning, adding that breakfast was not necessary. My name is Teresa Baek, she said.

The woman offered her a sturdy handshake. Call me Anna.

When the doors of Anna Gallo's *Lily* bed and breakfast finally re-opened in the spring of 1965, it was a lovely day, surprisingly warm for early April. The bloom of herbaceous plants was plentiful. The preservation of a new name, Gallo, in salutation to Anna's Italian father; the acquiescence of medieval times. Her watchdog and custodian.

There were two rooms on the ground floor – the kitchen, painted in mustard-yellow and a living room partitioned into a make-do seated breakfast area with four chequered tables and wonky wooden chairs. As she took to the narrow staircase, Teresa noticed a row of pale green parrots – eight in total in mid-flight, about to emigrate – porcelain, she thought. On the top floor, she was told, were Anna's private living quarters which intrigued her as apparently they were firmly locked. In the stairwell there was a single photograph of an elderly man, sitting, reading a book which she couldn't decipher the title of. He wore an old Aran jumper with holes at both elbows.

As they climbed to the landing, Teresa was shown one bathroom, a separate toilet and five bedrooms, each named respectively after prominent writers and artists: Dickens, Nicholson, Lawrence, Friedan and Dante, hanging awkwardly on each door from a rusty chain. Each room was betrothed with a manuscripted quotation. Some kind of reminder of who we are and where we come from perhaps, she mulled over. Teresa was assigned Betty Friedan's room, although, if truth be told, she would have preferred to have spent the night with Dickens. She racked her brains, trying to remember what the artist Nicholson was well known for. Ah yes, finally coming to her, his love of drawing and painting mushrooms.

Teresa had been brought up by her mother, a descendent of a wealthy merchant from the traditional village of Bukchon Hanok, never quite making it into the epitome of Seoul, but nevertheless, during her childhood, Teresa never remembered going without anything. Food was always sufficient, her clothes replaced six-monthly, her wispy hair tamed, but what she remembered most as she thought back to that time was the abundance of books. Their entire three-storey apartment was laden with books, old and new: manuscripts, novels, encyclopaedias, plays, sheet music and maps – lots and lots of maps. These all belonged to her English father who had died when Teresa was thirteen. Books were lined in alphabetical order, but it was the works of the French writer and essayist Simone de Beauvoir that she particularly applauded, how she wrote so forthrightly about the nature of women. And when she looked back at her father now, she was reminded of what he gifted her with – that incomparable love for literature. He had always called her his *angel drop* and, being only a mere child, she had pondered over the word *drop*, but in *angel* she always saw an image of a spiritual messenger. And whenever she looked into a mirror, she saw someone quite beautiful with deep green eyes and soft hazel waves barely brushing the shoulders, finished with a tincture of light.

Teresa's life had been stamped with the smell and warmth of the written page and there was never a day that she was without a book; they were her comfort – quite simply who she was. And so it was through literature and the indelible memories of her father that Teresa began to understand the merits of humankind; what had once impeded her had now been replaced by the reassuring presence of her father.

Teresa didn't leave directly the next morning; nor did she leave the following day, or the day after that, instead she stayed for some time and was at *Lily* to welcome the second guests on the morning of Friday June 10th. There was little pomp or ceremony, just fresh lilies placed on the shelves aside the front door. Teresa had woken early and was helping Anna prepare breakfast as the new guests were soon to be expected. There was colour outside though. The ground and trees were covered in a silver coating of dew, but it was the sun that gave it brightness, a sheen that reminded them both that preparations were being made for new growth and hopes for a different future. The good life.

Chapter 2

1957

Anna Gallo had lived in a humdrum part of West Yorkshire – a little too far from the Colne Valley and definitely not close enough to the fifteenth-century village of Golcar with all its rich history – for most of her life. Why? Most people would ask. A place so unlike the emblem of Golcar's Lily, the celebration of religious iconography, that no one ever made the premeditated visit, nor did they, for the most, just simply come across it. It was plain. A place like Anna herself. Very much in need of resurrection. She had had hopes for change and that her home town would one day metamorphose into a flourishing 'Italian' rebirth with winding streets that led to a fistful of surprises and anonymous lanes; a maze for discovery; the antithesis of a Pandora box; a special mention in the Domesday survey perhaps; a place proud of its manor house, weaver cottages and textile industries like so many neighbouring villages and towns were. This had not been the case for Anna.

So, together with the exigency of residents who had long disappeared like melting snow, Anna's homestead was clearly no Italian Riviera, unlike some of its rival villages, with their flowing hillsides, enthusiastic tourists, foragers, wanderers and genteel types. There were no Italian summers here for Anna, where warmth blew casually from all directions, no need for afternoon siestas, or squares with **cacio al fuso** and bocce being played; instead, a cold wind attacked from all angles, straight from the north upon the hilly terrain.

As a child, Anna had likened herself to the lily of Golcar when her father had read his own made-up regales of white lilies, of Hera and Zeus, of hope and goodness. And on a visit to London with her great-aunt Martha, she had stood in front of the painting *Carnation, Lily, Lily, Rose* and had always been reminded of the magic of those flowers, the happiness on the children's faces and the idea of make-believe. A childhood depiction she remembered to this very day.

Unfortunately, there was no one to share those memories with. A mere seventy-six inhabitants had remained in this West Yorkshire anomaly, all but a handful ripened now in old age and already on their way to the stripped cemetery, which surfaced at the very summit of the moor. Inauspicious, enigmatic, odd. Even the native birds had flocked to newer horizons. But Anna had remained. Alone.

With help from her father's will, she had then made the valorous (though Anna would not have described herself a hero, just yearning for something different) decision in 1964 to relocate, this time slightly closer to Golcar, but not really that close at all, and set up her own lodgings – a new bed and breakfast – and call it *Anna Gallo's Lily*.

Oh yes, the 1960s – the decade of liberalism, the time for change and hope, the emancipation of women, civil rights, the burning of bras – free love! In her dreams it was to be a magical place with a garden full of papery lanterns (honouring Singer Sargent), scents of Japanese lilies, rich yellow gardenias, pink roses, jasmine, lavender and honeysuckle, with the Italian touch, and in early summer, bougainvillea to welcome the guests as they crossed her threshold, with their calm and happy expressions. She had chosen a ramshackle of a weaver's cottage to live in, on the husk of a hill, overlooking deep into a valley, where she would lay the foundations of her bed and breakfast.

She had taken very little with her – a few pieces of furniture, an old school trunk and her father's trilby hatbox. The trunk had belonged to her mother. She would not be surprised by what her mother had kept there, but the hatbox was a delight. Secrets her father had kept from his wife. *Dear old Papa*, Anna always said out loud; his jar of Vaseline which he had always soothingly applied to her toes after he had wrapped her tight with a bath towel, pretending to send her off, addressed, stamped and posted. He would then place her high on his shoulders and the two of them would look into the Dickensian looking-glass and describe what they saw – she was his *poppy*, sensitive as a butterfly, with almost white hair, so flaxen in its tone, and the single, misplaced curl skirting her forehead. She would touch his mop of jet-black hair, slightly unkempt and greying to the sides, and his Mediterranean-bronzed complexion which she would later inherit, but it was his bushy eyebrows Anna liked most of all which made him look like a Bactrian camel, without the mascaraed eyelashes. They would play at making silly faces at each other like in the Hall of Mirrors at fairgrounds and they would laugh until the pits of their stomachs ached. And he would always repeat the same question, *and what do you want to become when you grow up poppy?* And she would answer in the same way, *to make people happy.*

She found ten bottles of unopened Old Spice; unused birthday presents from her mother; a half-used bar of Wrights soap, which he loved – its pungent smell that stuck to his skin; an empty bottle of Johnson's Baby Powder (Anna's favourite smell); an empty packet of Player's cigarettes, his favourite brand; a tiny abridged copy of all Shakespeare's tragedies, which he almost knew word for word; a beautifully embossed copy of Blake's *Songs of Innocence*, reading and re-reading *The Little Girl Lost* to Anna at bedtime throughout her childhood and continuing reading together into adulthood; and the four moth-eaten Aran sweaters, which he changed into, alternating between each of them every evening as he returned home from work. She remembered their unplanned walks over the moors and the expression on her mother's face when they returned with mud-trodden boots, dirtying the polished parquet. She remembered how her father winked covertly at her as they changed footwear and darted to the local for bacon sarnies.

Anna left the old school trunk alone. Unopened.

Anna had also found a bundle of unexpected letters, deep inside the hatbox's lining, all opened and now sepia in colour, drawn together by ribbon. There were three in total. She had thought this incongruous. She undid the loosely tied ribbon and began reading … the letters, all short and clearly copies of their originals with their slightly smudgy appearance, written on just a single page. Two of which were written in her father's hand and signed with his customary *AM* to names of people Anna neither knew nor recognised. The third and remaining letter was not signed by her father, but by someone named Chance and she thought the signature over-elaborate. She wondered, then, whether she had really known everything about her papa.

The first letter was short in its sentiment; Anna deciphered that a woman named Marybeth had sent her father a short collection of poetry, written in deep iambic tetrameter, lines irregularly halved, quartered, dissected. Poems that seemed to be all about mushrooms. The final sentence was straightforward and neutral in its tone. 'After careful consideration, we will be unable to publish your collection.'

The third letter was a little lengthier and somewhat mysterious in its content. 'We do not know each other personally, but my brother, Oliver, seems to have had some connection with you. After a long illness, he sadly died last year and on reading his will he had made mention of you, having sent you his memoirs, *The Joys of the Bourgeoisie*. You never responded.' Signed, as said, Chance with an RSVP address centred at the top of the page. Once again, she noted the elegant script.

The second letter was written to a Mr Stan Biggs and a Master Stan Biggs. It was the briefest of all three. 'I thank you for sending us *The Essential Guide to Coffee Manufacturing*. Following our editorial team's deliberation' – the formal tone of which Anna recognised to be her father's – 'on this occasion, with regret we have to inform you that you have been unsuccessful.'

Anna inhabited the top floor of her bed and breakfast – one bathroom, one bedroom. Mid-level was assigned to a maximum of five guest rooms, a bathroom, and one guest toilet. On the ground floor there was a small kitchen and adequately sized breakfast-cum-living room, which Anna renamed her parlour. Two of the bedrooms were large and homed three single beds, one washbasin, somewhat rusted. The other three bedrooms were just large enough for a single bed. She had had to spend all her savings on electrical and construction work – there had been no functional boiler or adequate lighting, and dangerous wiring, rot and termites had invaded all floors, and she had to re-lay the bedrock to prevent any further subsidence. These were just jobs that had to be fixed without the funds needed for any cosmetic surgery; just jobs that needed righting. As a result, there was nothing of note to write home about in terms of finesse or decoration, but she had retained the weaver's handlooms, the stoned floors, the thatched gable roof and the original fireplace. There was the odd dried bunch of musky lilacs and tulips and the odd displaced ornament. Nothing notable. Nothing to write home about.

Each bed had identical candlewick eiderdowns (bought as a job lot) in mottled green and blue angular squares which if stared at for too long had an unintended hypnotising effect. There were half-eaten wooden wardrobes in the larger rooms, acned by *wood borers, and* single bedside cupboards with the same problem in the smaller rooms. Psychedelic rugs differing in size haphazardly covered the badly stained floorboards. This always made Anna smile though, as she thought of how her grandma had a knack of staining her blouses with all sorts of spillages – due, she thought, to her oversized bosom – so a brooch was pinned to her and moved around her chest accordingly. The kitchen was painted in mustard-yellow, the vogue of the time, matching the reliable Aga. All the walls matched the shared bathroom, painted in the popular avocado green and the Frigidaire stood slightly lopsided, having lost one foot, leaning against the backdoor. Anna had to keep reminding herself that although not perfect, there were grounds for hope.

With so little experience, she pictured arriving guests signing her white satin guestbook, maybe removing their footwear, and being handed a key to be used at their disposal, and reminded, for those without transportation, to return by ten-thirty p.m. if they were planning to go out for the evening as that was the time the last local bus ran. But of course this, she knew, would be a rarity, as the closest town only had one coffee establishment, serving curly cucumber sandwiches and week-old doughnuts with their insides left out, and closed its doors at four sharp in the afternoon. There were no restaurants as such, just a rundown public house at the edge of town which on a good day sold packets of out-of-date salt-and-vinegar crisps and peanuts and flat ale.

But then there was Anna's *Lily*.

Although somewhat penniless now, she had promised herself that her bed and breakfast would one day be notable, worthy of her Italian-descent homemade Venetian ciabatta, thinly massaged with oil, garlic, freshly grown plum tomatoes, a plethora of cured meats and a delicate selection of fruit, chosen only for its utter ripeness. But for now, in those early days, she might have to turn a little to some of the British gastronomy, just to try and conjure up punters. Two pork sausages, a slither of black pudding, smothered with tinned Heinz baked beans, two measly dried-up mushrooms which had lost all their juiciness from being scrubbed and washed too many times. And finally the shrivelled bacon, over-salted, laid upon Mother's Pride three-day-old sliced white. This was not what Anna had envisioned. She liked the idea though that those who had stayed showed an openness and honesty when making their exchange and hoped that what they had to say was not too harsh, but would alert her to change. But in the early days, they had often read a little bit like this: *basic, some original features maintained, quaint, a little draughty, musty, acceptable, Anna is welcoming and happy to please, beautiful local scenery a fair drive away, breakfast was really nothing special, hard to quite describe this place – sorry …* and so on.

Chapter 3

Resurrection of 1964

With savings from her emerging income, aided by twelve months of frugal living, Anna spent long days steeped in horticultural encyclopaedias; she employed a gardener to help her build a miniature Italian garden, a pergola with evergreen topiary dotted purposefully, a small water feature, herbs in terracotta pots and symmetrical cypress shrubbery. She employed an Italian chef to teach her the fineries of bread-making, a charcutier to teach her how to cure her own ham, oil producers to teach her to distil the finest Italian extra virgin oils from producers in Lucca, Perugia, and Montevarchi, and interior designers to advise her on the interior facelift. Although this was never fully accomplished as she ran out of funds midway through, Anna knew that one day it would be.

Her photographic memory had come to good use, a handy skill pointed out to her by her favourite class two teacher, a Mrs Gee. When Anna had joined the school mid-year, she was turning nine and had taken an instant liking to Mrs Gee. She had thought her old – in fact she was only thirty-one, but for a nine-year-old, this was old. But age, Anna had always thought, was an overrated concept anyway. It was her soft voice that Anna was drawn to most, a calmness about her that she was unused to, having a mother that always spoke at the top of her voice, bickering throughout the day. Mrs Gee was more like her father. She offered her serenity.

Mrs Gee always dressed as a teacher should: laced black highly polished shoes, a tweed skirt throughout the year (whatever the weather) and an assortment of lightly coloured shirts, dependent on the day of the week. Mondays and Wednesdays were pale yellow. It was pastel green for Tuesdays, and on Thursdays, pale turquoise. But on Fridays, she risked a stronger amber-yellow to mark the holy day, and whenever Anna thought about Friday's colour, she would giggle inside because that very colour was the exact same as the oil used for the burnt chips and over-fried plaice they were served on Fridays: burnt exterior, gooey inside, like an imperfectly made macaroon.

Anna sat at her oak kitchen table. In front of her lay the three letters she had come across in her papa's hatbox, and it was then that she decided that Marybeth, Mr and Master Biggs, and Chance would be her next guests, taking four of the rooms, and would without hesitation vivify the very foundations of this establishment. She would keep the fifth room ready for the odd passer-by (this would end up being Teresa's). She wrote a single letter to each of them, inviting them to join her in the grand opening of *Lily* and posted them that evening. She added a postscript, promising that their five-day stay would be worthwhile.

So after a long, onerous year, Anna lay on her

reupholstered settee, drank her evening tea of peppermint leaves freshly picked, finished the penultimate chapter of *The Pleasures of Italian Cooking* and sent herself off to bed.

Waiting for the first guest to arrive.

Chapter 4

Anna's life had been a succession of ups and downs with some middle bits. Firm decisions made, impulsive resolutions kept, hopes materialised, intuition inspired, broken marriages, promises kept, and rash commitments. Oh, yes, Anna was a one-in-a-million kind of lass that was for sure.

Anna's Italian father, Alberto Messina (the ancestral family name), had been a successful book publisher. He'd worked hard. Each day he set off to his office in the heart of Naples, but only after he had prepared Anna's breakfast of bread and jam, cocoa milk, biscuits, and dropped her off at school. She remembered the smell of polished wood on the panelling of his desk; his quill pen; photographs of her at play, her first day at school; their weekend walks; sharing a pizza oozing with melted mozzarella with the hint of taleggio. It was then no surprise that she had inherited his love of work, his optimism, and she recalled the times he returned home laden with new manuscripts which he was always so excited about, telling her all about the young writers eager to share their stories, enthusiastic poets personifying their first loves, biographies craving to be told, mystery writers, writers of fantasy absorbed in make-believe.

Her English-cum-South Korean mother on the other hand only wanted Anna to marry young like herself, whilst her father encouraged her studies and hoped one day, she might also work in the world of books. On Saturdays they would rummage in the local libraries, visit old bookshops in search for treasure, peruse in a café drinking weak cappuccinos, books in hand. And even when Anna's mother had made the family move from Italy to England when she was six, he had always found a way to find books. Anna's two grown-up siblings were settled in jobs in Palermo and remained there. Clara, an established accountant and Marco, a pioneering engineer. On the day of the move, trunk-loads of books were hoarded onto a lorry, alongside her mother's tapestried suitcases full of needless clothes and minor accessories.

Anna's mother was, by no stretch of the imagination, a taskmaster, at least when it came down to Anna, busy preparing her for married life. During each summer holiday, Anna's time was never her own. Language teachers were employed, seamstresses, music teachers, table dressers, deportment experts and entertaining gurus. No surprise then that Anna's mother's parents had been no different. They had brought Anna's mother up in exactly that same way. Children were supposed to keep their mouths firmly shut and just 'do'. They rarely visited and on the rare occasions they did, Anna was, in truth, ignored.

Anna sometimes felt that her English and Italian ancestry was a collection of bits and pieces, like a patchwork quilt or jigsaw puzzle which never quite fitted. Perhaps, she had always thought, it was this misshapen piece that she needed to find. And she had this very thought when she finally opened the doors of *Lily* in 1965.

When she was old enough, Anna escaped her mother's regime but always spent her Wednesday evenings and weekends with her father right up until his death. Neither had wanted to break their tradition. She found herself a part-time job in a library, cataloguing Victorian literature and then moved on to modern literature and poets from the 1900s. For her, it was a dream job, spending each lunch break reading whatever she could, whilst the other librarians ate their boxed lunches in the library canteen or in a local café. She scanned the shelves for children's fairy tales. Although probably a little too old now, she still loved the stories of Hans Christian Andersen, the dark tales of the Brothers Grimm, Antoine De Saint-Exupéry's enchanting illustrations in *The Little Prince*, and the very soul of *The Happy Prince*, daydreaming of being saved by knights in shining armour. She then dabbled in all sorts of jobs: working for a local biographer editing her lengthy manuscripts, writing a column for the *Daily Post*, only read by a few. She even had a stint as an assistant in a local 'modern' art gallery which had newly opened, but soon became bored as only a handful of visitors ever came in. She took courses in creative writing, the poets of the Middle Ages, Shakespeare's comedies and tragedies, book-binding, restoration, botany, flower arranging, and sourdough baking. And so, the list went on.

Chapter 5

1965 – Big Stan (Lawrence) and Little Stan (Dickens)

Stanley woke to the ring of his alarm clock. Six sharp. He could hear his father preparing breakfast downstairs. The first smell of the morning was always coffee. He grabbed his clothes, dressed quickly and joined his father in the dining room. The mahogany table, as usual, was well laid out, with an array of sweet pastries, *arepas, huevos pericos* and *pandebono* and his unfinished wooden jigsaw puzzle. No words were spoken until they both heard the horn of the car.

We must add here, reader, that Stanley's father was usually the best of sleepers, and nothing had ever managed to interrupt this ritual. Except, though, for the past three nights his sleep had been punctuated with repeated pictures of his son celebrating his future career, wearing his graduation gown surrounded by academics and friends so real in the detail. So hard to believe when he looked at him sitting in the back of the car, meek and mild. So instead of waking cantankerous as he would have expected, on those three mornings he was especially good-humoured, each image fixed like glue in his mind: the luminosity of light, the candles lit, the cake taking centre stage as Little Stan (now grown big, but forever referred to with the diminutive) and his friends enter with a distinctive dulcet sound. Twenty perfectly straightened tapered domes atop the tiers of gooey colour. He comes in – stopping all motion, bursting with pride, dressed in academic regalia. He takes his position at the head of the table – giving himself to his waiting guests, and slowly blowing each of the twenty candles out one by one. The love for a child so kindled within.

Images that he did not want to be broken or forgotten.

The journey from Bournemouth to Yorkshire would take five hours. Stanley sat in the back. Stanley Senior up front, talking enthusiastically to Branshaw, his assistant-cum-chauffeur-cum-everything. Stanley could only hear muffled parts of their conversation: it's a place I have always wanted to ... the windswept mornings and ... the fresh air ... I know a few days away will help ... And then, I received a letter from a ... inviting me to the opening ... Lily ... The decision had been clinched.

Stanley was confused, but he loved his father very much and trusted him, but also knew he would never inherit his zest for life. And his father knew that too and he also knew that it was his wife that his son took after. Jane had been an intelligent woman and when they married at the tender age of seventeen, he also knew that his new bride had only five years of her life left, at the very best. She had loved Yorkshire and would have been happy to settle there, but she also respected her husband's tenacity. When their son was born in the second year of their marriage, she chose to spend all her time at home seeing to his needs. When he was barely nine months old, she would read out loud from medicine journals written by colleagues she used to work with, piece together wooden jigsaw puzzles she had kept from her childhood which Stanley had a particular penchant for, and take him out each day in his stroller to pick wild blackberries and strawberries. But giving birth weakened her immunity and she died prematurely three days after Stanley's first birthday.

As Anna stood alongside Teresa to welcome the second guests, with slight disquietude, a large man walked self-assuredly towards them ahead of a small fragile boy.

Much later, maybe years after they had left, these guests were secretly renamed by Teresa and Anna as Big Stan and Little Stan, not doppelgangers, but father and son. The father was a somewhat stout man in his mid-sixties, Teresa surmised. He carried with him a provincial accent from the north yet with the hue of Spanish and when he spoke it was the strong sense of loquacious pride he elicited that Teresa was intrigued by. Stan was a coffee maker, a distiller and entrepreneur, a skill that he had acquired and shared with his father and grandfather, and had first learned the trade as a youngster during the Great War in Columbia. It was said that the producer of his bean derived from Café Granja La Esperanza, who were known to cultivate the finest espresso. However, Stan had channelled his tastes by changing the texture and taste of his espresso, and was watched, while he worked, by all his admirers, shadowing his every movement as he tightened the spout, rotated the burrs, continually adjusting and re-adjusting, checking for humidity and not until the temperature was perfected by tamping his ground coffee in slow motion – only then was his cortado ready to serve. With a slightly vexed expression, he added that he had had to succumb to serving espressos with just the splash of milk, cappuccinos, and – on Friday afternoons only – he relented to making his much-detested latte.

He carried only an unusually shaped suitcase which he unwrapped in the same way as if he was undressing a fragile woman or mending the wing of a dove: diligently, methodically and caressingly. This was his heirloom – the ancient, untainted cafetera. Master Stan, however, had the arduous task of carrying their other larger, rectangular suitcase, which showed all the signs of age. Anna noticed that the boy seemed neither stout nor proud, but rather wafery and elf-life in his disposition as he slouched forth. Master Stan was ten years old and still a schoolboy. Both women wondered as to why he wasn't at school, but never directed those thoughts to either one.

The boy was indeed placid, his complexion similar to a weakening light bulb in need of replenishment. His clothes, also pale, loosely covered his body; snippets of bony limbs protruded when he occasionally crossed his legs and his collar bone flickered when he indulged in conversation, which was rare. His father was the talker. The boy's companion was his dictionary which never seemed to leave his side. He perpetually fluttered the pages like a moth and always seemed scared someone or something was about to trample on him.

It emerged that the reason for him not being schooled was that on his second day as a junior, a new geography teacher had joined the school. Mutterings about her severity permeated throughout the school and it seemed that even the stern head teacher was wary of Mrs Coleridge. With her close-set eyes and touch of indentation like an etcher's burr, and twisted manner, she had cruelly confiscated Stan's one companion (his dictionary), and in front of the class had torn out each of the pages one by one – the remnants of which he later found tossed into the roadside outside the school gates. Tyre marks and afternoon drizzle had obliterated every page. This was the last day of Stan's formal education. But Mrs Coleridge was not the only teacher to have affected him. There had been Mr Chadwick, a chemistry teacher nearing the end of his long teaching career. It felt for Stan that this departure was being solely blamed upon his students, namely Little Stan. Being his final term, the panic of his reluctant retirement had become all too apparent. He would batter Stan with his disconcerting remarks like the constant pounding when butterflying a chicken, and to top that, his constant frown deployed utter disapproval. There had also been the time when Stan first entered his primary school and been cornered by a group of older girls questioning him on all levels: the length of his hair, which movies he liked best, could he read fluently, was his handwriting any good? Question after question, until they dispersed, before attacking another novice. He had fantasised on so many occasions of how he could have been a very different type of person – strong and defiant, but passionate, just like his father – and had to some degree accepted his lot, but these fantasies kept returning, resilient.

Those, he transcribed and hid away, not wanting anyone to find them, especially his father.

I was in a place so familiar but had hated. I had expected to see the memory recrudesce – the defaced book with its wet tyre marks still lying still by the gates. Instead, my dictionary shone as it always had, but had grown three-fold, heavy with companionship. I picked it up almost in slow motion, instead of the expected weight, it was light. I entered by the main school double-door with an upright gait having once passed through this dreaded playground, and walked the two flights of stairs, passing the chemistry room into Mrs Coleridge's geography class. No poor, meek students; just her, marking papers, head bent down with her usual twisted demeanour. And now, just before lifting, the weightlessness had turned heavy; I lifted it high and dropped it hard onto her desk. I turned and left.

So, was it any wonder that home-schooling suited Stan perfectly? With Ms Lore, Mr Macpherson and Mrs Courtney, Stan had been given the education he deserved.

Teresa warmly invited them to the kitchen table where Anna sat pouring tea into her fine china cups which, although cracked, were still elegantly dressed with rose heads and lily stalks. Anna noticed Mr Stan's expression change, from a timbre of badinage to the accord of seriousness, as he saw the insipid brownish colour of the tea being poured and withdrew only to return minutes later with another of his prized possessions: an air-dried box of freshly ground beans. Without a word he began to percolate his espresso slowly, drip by rich drip painting the interior of each of his tiny white cups which his son handed to him in automatic motion. Both Anna and Teresa watched him move his arms, sending the rich aroma around the room, like cheery French lavender in cantillation.

It was only at that moment that the boy looked up briefly at both women and noticed the older woman's – called Anna – hands were grubby like Avril's (his mother's younger sister who no one ever mentioned) always were, whose fingernails also had a fine line of grit which seemed as though etched on and never disappeared. This had always mystified him, as the rest of her was so pristine and always smelt recently washed. What he did like, though, was the woman Anna's patchwork shawl because it looked to him like jigsaw pieces coated in fur.

In harmony, father and son softly hummed to the harmonic melodies of an old Spanish folk song, the score of the scratch of the guacharaca and the multi-layered timbres of an accordion which Teresa recognised, and once again, she was brought back to her learned father and the air became thick with undoubting love.

Teresa couldn't help joining in with the final hummed silence.

The expression of both as deep as the waft of earthiness enveloping the room, with no question of hesitation or doubt, as if in a trance Anna and Teresa sipped the delights from Columbia. This was the way it had begun and that evening Teresa noticed Anna empty the contents of her once beloved tea caddy directly into the bin, her tribute to *The Essential Guide to Coffee Manufacturing*. She kept the caddy for sentimental reasons.

Anna led the father to the Lawrence room, whilst Teresa took the boy to the Dickens room. And, for her, she sensed they would become firm friends. She, with her books, him, with his dictionary. The perfect marriage.

Breakfast was a plateau of fruit: blackberries, cherries, cranberries, strawberries, alongside a plateau of cracked pepper crackers, yolkless omelettes, granola aside a small jug of creamy milk, rhubarb muffins, and herbal tea, which gave off the faint smell and look of silage. Anna was clearly bemused, Teresa less so, but his expression gave off such a tinge of pleasurable delight. This had been all Master Stan's work, being a nemesis of anything yellow in colour (the reasons why no one seemed to know). But it wasn't just food that posed problems for him; his aversion to yellow affected all walks of his young life. It was in the daffodils, the buttercups, the sun on a particularly sunny day, in the pigment of paint, in the ochres of paintings, on furnishings, the dye in clothes, in the colour of one's hair …

Mr Stan watched his son explain that in the larger suitcase there was a plethora of what he described as 'optional delights'. They were to become good friends, thought Little Stan's father, quietly pleased that, at long last, Stan had found a soulmate.

At breakfast, Big Stan brought up the question of Anna's letter.

Chapter 6

Love, Marriage and Romance

Anna's parents had been mere teenagers when they married after a whirlwind of an engagement planned predominately by their respective parents. A planned nuptial should we say. Anna's Italian grandfather and her English grandmother had been at school together and had remained distant friends; at least that was what her mother had thought. She had never been a good reader of character. So that was that. They married. The wedding was a modest affair. He was twenty-one, she, just turning twenty. No love, a little affection. To others though, they seemed the perfect couple.

Anna's family had been affluent with no shortage of money or basic resources. With both of her parents out at work, at the tender age of eight, Anna had found herself with an independence she was neither aware of nor understood. Her two older siblings spanned fifteen years between them – her sister, Joselyn, ten years her senior and brother, Lucas, fifteen. She was, by all reasonable deduction, alone. An only child.

Along with the tutelage, when Anna was alone, she would find lists sellotaped to the fridge door, left by her mother with a list of household chores for the day. During the school term, it was barely any shorter, and on the weekends, much longer. On Saturdays, she had to prepare the evening meal, which she never minded as she saw this not as a task, but as a welcoming reprieve – her father's favourite, and which also reminded her mother of their union, was homemade orzo, served in the traditional way, known as the Italian 'wedding' soup, made using green vegetables, beef and pork meatballs. Her mother never cooked and never cleaned. She felt it was beneath her. Chores that involved cooking, low and slow, preparing meats, de-boning fish, scrubbing potatoes and chopping, hoovering, drip-drying, scrubbing and polishing seemed a fool's errand. Anna remembered the lack of warmth in those harsh notes and had always felt as though she was one of her mother's many minions. Not her daughter.

On her ninth birthday, she remembered unwrapping her first hard-covered book, small and dressed in navy, embossed in glistening white, a gift from her father. It was called *Songs of Innocence* and he had recited his favourite poem *The Land of Dreams* and had made a point to remind her that the 'boy' in the poem meant girls too! And it was this collection of poems that had become her new best friend, her companion, her compatriot, her confidante, her Northern star …

And it had been that deep sonority of reflected lilies that had always been Anna's very favourite image.

Anna's mother died at home, unexpectedly, in 1961. The post-mortem revealed nothing – finally reaching a verdict of 'died from natural causes'. For one entire year, Anna and her papa had enjoyed a wonderful, uninterrupted life together, and then in the summer he had died after a long fight with throat cancer. Anna had been by his bedside reciting Blake's *The Little Girl Lost*.

Anna, though, yearned for a very different kind of match. Not a neutral one, but a union full of commitment. She had always dreamt of true romance, spurred on by the books of Aurelia Stowe and Montgomery's *Anne of Green Gables*. Although she loved her papa dearly, he had never taught her the intricacies of love and her mother never once broached the subject. All she had ever learned from school during Mr Coates' biology lessons was the reproductive organs of other mammals, how to dissect a worm and a couple of lessons on the digestive system. So, was it no wonder that when she left school, although perfectly qualified, she wasn't at all in the art of love and espousal. She noticed that what few friends she did have were either engaged or in serious relationships. There had been Tommy Shield who had also gone to the same school and like Anna was studious – occasionally they would walk home together, share a cream bun, discuss homework assignments, cram for upcoming exams. So when Tommy plucked up the courage to ask her to the end of year prom, Anna accepted. At the end of the evening, he had kissed her full-mouthed, slobbering his tongue across her teeth until she drew away, gasping for breath. And that put an end to that.

Lionel Falconer appeared next, ten years Anna's senior. Anna liked his maturity, his steady job, his anchored countenance. It was his strange expression when he was thinking – his right eye would begin twitching and the vein on his balding head would quiver, which reminded Anna of a twittering flamingo. This liaison lasted two months.

And then followed two marriages; the first of which was to a Samuel Moreau – an Italian. Perfect, she thought.

Unassuming and honest, Samuel was a writer, a biographer and fairly well thought of, with three successful publications behind him and starting number four. They had met in a theatre foyer. They had been drawn together by a mutual friend over a glass of chilled Pinot Grigio. Then followed a succession of dates and Anna felt she was truly in love, so when Samuel proposed to her one year later over a glass of Pinot Grigio, she accepted without hesitation. Things changed almost immediately. Any free time they did have, Anna would find Samuel slumped in his writing study, sometimes unable to speak, tears rolling down his face and he would remain there, alone for days on end. The marriage ended in a swift divorce eighteen months later. When Anna met Jack Jackson, three years later in a Yorkshire tearoom, they happened to end up having to share the same table. Anna was drinking a local blend of her favourite tea. Jack was finishing an over-creamed scone. She liked the way the cream caught the sides of his mouth and remained there. She loved his shaggy, slightly greying hair, reminding her of a Beatrix Potter character. She liked the stain on his Aran jumper and the frayed seams of his trousers. It was only his name she was unsure about. Maybe it was a family joke? They touched on a few patent subjects – the weather, the climate, the cost of living. Just the ordinary things of life. Her surety suggested meeting up again the following week. So, for the next three months, every Thursday afternoon, they would meet in the tearoom enjoying each other's company. It was two months later, Jack suggested he cook her a meal, his speciality, a giant Yorkshire pudding filled with meat and gravy. And there, their romance began. Their first kiss without the slobbering, gentle and pleasant, filled Anna with a fizziness she had never experienced before. They married late spring the following year as soon as the first Asiatic lilies bloomed. Everything seemed perfect. The marriage lasted a wonderful three years and only ended when Jack died from a disease he had been diagnosed with long before he had met Anna, but had kept secret from her. Everything, she thought, had been left to *chance* like the risks associated with that said card in the game of Monopoly.

Anna remained single, without regret. She felt she had learned a little more about the male species, a little more about love, a little more about how they tick, how this collective hybrid conjectured, chose to dress and what their culinary interests were. Not a whole lot more, except that Jack Jackson, with that funny name, had taught her a little more about love.

Chapter 7

1965 – Marybeth (Nicholson)

The fourth guest was named Marybeth.

Marybeth was a solitary figure, having neither siblings nor children of her own; her mother dead. Unexpectedly. Her father, so refined with the gentlest of natures, had died unforeseen, sometime prior. Marybeth had grown used to the company of her five dogs, a brew of breeds, colours, behaviours, likes and dislikes: a lazy Welsh Corgi who was partial to strawberry jam, nocturnal twin terriers, an Airedale Terrier who refused to leave the house, taking on the airs of an aristocrat, and a somewhat yellowed golden retriever who was a self-elective mute. Living on the boundary of the market town of Huddersfield, her immediate surroundings became her domain, a sky so low, suffocating and murky of cloud. This wasn't a matter of like or dislike for her, just a blatant fact. The 'hikikomori' was the title given to her by those who caught a rare glimpse and this nickname had lingered with her. Her culinary skills were limited. She had no interest in food beyond its means for sustenance. Yet, there had been many, many times this hadn't been the case, times when she had loved. Times when she had assembled the most lavish of meals for loved ones. Now with all that regality dissipated, like a dethroned queen, and that lavishness stripped away, she constructed plain cheese sandwiches and fried a mushroom or two, but that was about it. So, apart from her dogs which she had named by number only, from one to five (being averse to any suggestion of cuteness), she was inclined towards the art of foraging – specifically, for mushrooms. Particularly those of the rarest quality: Cortinarus rubellus, Amanita phalloides, and the Destroying Angel, with their pure white rounded heads. It was the death cap that intrigued her most, the idea of beauty being so deadly, but tasting ordinary. So on a good day it was the finding of these mushrooms that gave Marybeth the most pleasure and satisfaction. There was indeed nothing she didn't know about the simple mushroom. She had even written a short collection of poetry in homage to the species and sent it to a prominent Italian publisher, an Alberto Messina.

It must be said though, that Marybeth was a little bit of a Mrs Malaprop, probably as a result of conversing too long with dogs, numbers and mushrooms. Indeed, she had her own way of speaking, inflected with a hint of Latin.

She had heard that nearby, there was a place said to have the most unusual mushrooms for those in the know – hidden deep under the trunks of aged old oak and beech trees. In her thoughts, she imagined herself coming home with a treasure of Bûche de Noël, packed tightly into her knapsack, and unpacking each one slowly and caressingly, classifying and manicuring them with surgical gloves.

She reckoned she could make the four-hour journey partly by the local bus and partly on foot, but would probably have to spend one night in a bed and breakfast or something. This filled her with dread. It had been so long since she had spent the night in a stranger's house or for that matter been to a restaurant, gone on holiday, watched a film or been to the theatre, met informally with friends in a café, toasted birthdays, anniversaries, or any celebration. But, as she pictured the opportunity to catch this prize, she decided with unlikely intuition she would leave the following evening as night set in, remaining inconspicuous, but more importantly, the sun rising is the ideal time for a forager – uninterrupted and she had read somewhere this is when the mushrooms appear as *little lanterns*. This was her plan.

She spent the following day preparing, slightly mindful of the five dogs, leaving enough food and water for five days and access for their toiletry needs, just in case of mishap. And at teatime she set off. The journey took a little longer though: the last bus broke down without a replacement, and she had to make the remaining leg of the journey on foot – a much more taxing walk at that. She finally arrived at Bank Wood just three hours past midnight. She located the perfect oaks and beyond, there were clusters of beeches just waiting to be hunted. It was so much easier than she had first imagined and in less than three hours, her knapsack was full to the brim. Whether it was the smile behind Marybeth's smirk or the pull of her filled knapsack, she was no doubt pleased with her endeavour.

Then, on to the harder, more desirous task of where to spend the night? She walked a little way and came across an old weaver's cottage, slightly disgruntled and not at all ostentatious. She peered through the dimly lit kitchen and noticed *The Pleasures of Italian Cooking* left face down on the table. She wondered what to do next, unaccustomed for so long to any kind of etiquette, so simply knocked once. A child, dressed in pyjamas, opened the door and in she went. The proprietor if you please, she uttered without harmony. An older woman appeared. Please come in. Have you made a booking? She explained her predicament and was led upstairs to a small room with a single wardrobe and bed.

On the landing, Teresa watched her carefully take off her knapsack and lay it down on the eiderdown. She also noticed her fingernails needed a good old scrub. Marybeth had no idea what to do next, so she closed the door and inspected her mushrooms, packed them away and then sat perched on the edge of the bed as though coming out of hypnosis until she heard muffled voices below. She picked up her knapsack and tiptoed downstairs so as not to be heard.

With the sun rising, spreading a fine haze across the threshold, she left. It was Anna that realised and caught her as she walked away. She called her back and asked her if she would like some breakfast before she made the journey homeward. After all, Anna preferred to get to know her guests just a little bit and there was something familiar about Marybeth. With some reluctance, Marybeth returned and was offered breakfast – a plate of cured ham, Italian bread and an English-style egg, served with Big Stan's manicured coffee. She stared intently at these offerings and simply wondered where the mushrooms were. After all what's breakfast without mushrooms, she thought to add, but didn't, instead, just enquired (for the sake of protocol) whether there were any mushrooms. And, thus began the topic of mushrooms, all so familiar to Marybeth. It was then that Anna knew she was the writer of the collection of poetry rejected by her father. There was no stopping Marybeth with her regard to mushrooms, her passion, fascination, knowledge, rhetoric, doting, intimacy; you could say her accounts were emblematic poignancy akin to a love affair, like floating two inches above the ground or holding a smile all day without ever noticing, or, as Anna thought back, like being in love.

In fact Marybeth stayed at *Lily* for the full five days – as did all the other guests – and spent her days foraging and her evenings talking about mushrooms, dogs and about being an only child. Shall we say, Anna and Marybeth grew closer, like confidantes, perhaps not quite soulmates yet, but that would come, she was sure of it.

Chapter 8

1965 – Chance (Dante)

Chance thought he would have just enough time for a quick one at the club, di membri privati. He was after all a person of molto importante. A shot of Campari perhaps, followed with a Spritz Veneziano. Of course, as was the way with Chance, one drink usually led to another and then another … he wasn't one for close friends, just acquaintances – people not to rely on, just to chat to over the mundane activities of life: the quality of the latest vintage, the opening of a new art gallery, the unveiling of a new masterpiece. Never politics, financial matters, or stocks and shares. These were of no interest to Chance. He had dabbled with the idea of becoming a writer and once had written to a leading publishing house, to the Italian director of course.

He had meant to set off in good time, driving to the airport, catching the afternoon flight to Manchester, picking up his privately hired car and onto West Yorkshire in three and a half hours. This didn't actually happen, one too many, missing his flight and having to take the evening flight instead.

He arrived at *Lily* in the middle of the night, too dark to see the spring flowers beginning to bloom. All was silent. Anna didn't hear the faint tintinnabulation of the brass bell, indistinct. He tried a few more times and then gave up. It was not until six-thirty the following morning that Anna noticed the stranger in a bundle lying to the left of the welcome mat. Please come, come in, she said with a knowing smile. He simply bade her *buongiorno*. Slightly bedraggled but dressed in a flamboyant kimono-styled outercoat, Chance crossed Anna's threshold. Teresa transfixed and with the thought of swashbuckling, bravado, theatre and great vivaciousness, was rekindled to the joshing days of Douglas Fairbanks and the light braggadocio in Mark of Zorro, discreetly smiling the faintest of smiles.

When Anna said that guests were free to have breakfast at any time from seven-thirty, Chance explained he had a number of allergies apart from being a strict vegan – no gluten, no wheat, no vegetables containing more than one fluid ounce of liquid, no stabilisers or additives – and then presented a double-sided printed version of this, listing a multitude of further disenables. He retired to the Dante room. This was the brother of the rejected author of *The Joys of the Bourgeoisie*. Anna knew.

Chance came from a family that lived their lives independent of each other, so no firm bonds were ever made, his parents getting on with things in opposite wings of the family estate. His mother spent her days entertaining others with her penchant for card games and dining out each evening chit-chatting and indulging her appetite. His father in the right wing spent every other day making sure his assets were in order – talking to bankers, lawyers, accountants. However, Chance never once saw him actually go out to work as such, although his older brother, Oliver, had informed him that he worked in 'property', which hadn't enlightened him one little bit. Chance had an older sister, fifteen years his senior, who had gone to Finishing School in Paris when she was seventeen and had never returned.

Chance had never really needed to work. He had dabbled with this and that, but as he was so well-endowed with enough money to last him a lifetime, coming in promptly every month via his now deceased parents, the motivation had never been there. Although it must be added that Chance had most definitely wanted a vocation, not for monetary reasons, he just wanted a purpose in life. Art and history had been his favourite subjects at school (receiving the only positive comments from his teachers), which led to a chain of loosely associated vocations and were all fleeting. He retrained as an archivist, became an art authenticator in forging (a particular interest of his), even a short period as a conservationist and was granted with a research fellowship, which seemed more about his wealth than his worth, but none of these suited him and none satisfied his needs.

Chance was a failed art historian – his own words – but he still awoke at six o'clock sharp every morning and took out his companion, his beloved typewriter, plumed in ivory keys that he cleaned with children's cotton buds each evening. He had published a couple of mediocre books on the lesser-known Venetian painters, but that had been more than twenty years ago, and since then, his 'writer's block' had become a thirty-foot wall – with no more than the odd word appearing lonely on the page. And with all the money in the world, nothing filled the gap of wordless pages. He was indeed a saddened man.

He divided his life between Venice and Vermont (he had a penchant for the letter V), paid for through the income from his family estate; in Italy, close to the San Zarracea church, he would stay at the fifteenth-century Cima Rosa. He loved the unassuming exterior of the church and with what was gained upon entering: its oversized sixteenth-century paintings adorning each wall. He would sit in deep contemplation with an espresso and a gluten-free Bussolà Buranello or bombolone, and then luncheon on cicchetti made from red artichokes or green olives. In the evenings, he would sit on the balcony sipping a local liqueur whilst looking down onto the statue-lined courtyard. Occasionally, he would meet up with friends, brush up on his Italian, but more usually, spend his time quietly reading and trying to write.

And in Vermont, summer through to October, he could watch autumn's rich foliage erupt in the family's one-hundred acre walled home set amongst olive trees and vine groves in the soul of its mosaic. The fall of golden leaves, the endless hills and valleys with mists rising from dawn, the picturesque blue rivers, reminiscent of a child's first painting. Here though, he was expected to be a little more social, perhaps entertain twice weekly, spend evenings with acquaintances, spoiled by his childhood nanny. But, over the weekends he would sit amongst the olive groves with his typewriter trying to conjure the words. Sometimes the aroma of his surroundings was enough, but more often than not, it wasn't.

Chapter 9

So, with all the guests arrived, the following days were spent adventuring, reading, debating, contemplating, admiring, observing, and puzzle-piecing. There was something quite strange, Anna thought, about the way all the guests seemed to have simply accepted each other as might be expected of close friends. It was as though they had always known each other. Anna kept these thoughts to herself, because, after all, it was just a feeling which needed mulling over. She decided to let time lapse and then she would perhaps understand their connection.

By the third day, relationships had surfaced. Anna noticed that Teresa would spend her days inside reading with offerings of help – preparing food, gardening, driving to the big supermarket in town, collecting errands for Anna. Big Stan seemed to love the company of Chance with his regular breakfast salutation of *che splendida festa* which didn't sound artificial but naturally avid. They spent hours walking and discussing the virtues of art and coffee, conjuring tenuous connections. But it was the growing companionship between

Marybeth and Little Stan that surprised her the most. They spent their mornings out, Anna had learned from Teresa; Marybeth would walk with Little Stan to the nearest wooded area and they would sit beneath an oak or beech – Stan with his dictionary, pen and pad, cogitating new found words, Marybeth with her knapsack loyal at her side prepared for any new discovery – and they would then return at teatime for English muffins and jammy scones (Anna never changed this traditional habit). Little Stan shared his ideas about ways to heighten the importance of the letter 'W' and unpacked his mother's old jigsaw puzzles and they would assemble together, laying out the pieces on the kitchen table. Anna thought this to be fortuitous.

So, as time went on, evenings were steeped in talk – chastising, sharing stories, joking and just being, and on the penultimate evening, they entertained each other with snippets from their lives, and it transpired that for Anna, important lessons had been learned. From Teresa, a long-lasting friendship together with the added gift of Jacobean language. From Big Stan, the cadence of coffee percolating, and from Little Stan, his latest ten-letter favourites, like *abaptiston, babblingly, nabobishly* and the purity of the dictionary and how to extend the discordant letter 'W'. From Chance, the merits of persistence and from Marybeth, the rewards of being an only child.

Chapter 10

Conversations

On the morning of day three, Chance, Big Stan, Marybeth and Little Stan arose before the light of day, before the songbirds sprang into action, and walked as young couples do down the wedding aisle, congregating between the elders and the lady's gloves with a certain air of mischief about them – rather like a diablerie or caper, or as Little Stan thought, schoolchildren in their Dahl-like roguishness. There were signs of great plans ahead, debating and serious regard directed for the most part by Marybeth in an uncharacteristic fashion, rather reminding Chance of a political activist he had once known in his college days, who had pervaded an edifying confidence within him. Even Little Stan found himself casting back to the time his mother had taken him to the synagogue to partake in Simchat Torah, solely a children's celebration of the annual reading of the Torah, and had heard the gaiety of the congregation, singing and dancing and the throwing of candy all over the children and had thought how he wished he was a Jew.

Yet, it was Chance's other flashback that suddenly came – the time he had only just entered puberty when his brother

Oliver was well into his twenties, having just finished his PhD on *The Glorification of British Symbolic Realism*. Chance had always seen his brother as an archangel, both literally and figuratively, but perhaps better framed as a child's *Angel of Art*, and although many of the words had made little sense at the time, he seemed to know exactly what was meant by each and every one of them. To Chance, his writing was sublime, unlike anything he knew he would come across again and he begged him to take him to London to see Singer Sargent's painting. On that journey Chance sat quietly, only pacified by Oliver's familiar twitch of the shoulder, his occasional flick of the hair and soft down of his cheek, but inside, he prickled all over and it was only when he had stood in front of *Carnation, Lily, Lily, Rose* that he had fully understood those once unfamiliar words which Oliver had written with such consummate beauty. They stood in semblance as Chance described the details within the painting – he saw the two little girls, twin-like, dressed in chorister's frills lighting the bellowed papery lanterns; he saw the full blooms of the tall white lilies and he saw the grassy verge, interrupted by daisies and delicate roses. That fine chasm between night and day.

And then, led by Little Stan as if in religious chorus, they formed a circle, catching the wispy dawn flicker as he recited six lines from his very first poem, unacknowledged with a simple Anon:

Lanterns, behold,
East meets west –
The dance of the fairies, pixies, sprites, sylphs and nymphs
Cast their symphonic delights;

Maidens and Masters come together and frolic

To the trumpets and horns that cry out to the joys of the spirits.

And the depiction of a newly planted floral bed was agreed by all – white carnations, Japanese mountain lilies and accents of pink roses.

And Chance was reminded once again of the dream he had had the previous night which he remembered image by image as though until its truth lay written by his own hand early that final day.

I saw the nebulous shadow of a figure looking to the south across the undistinguishable visage. A man, I thought, walking unsteadily towards me as though a child learning the rudimentary movements of walk. Still distant, there was some familiarity, features, the modest distinguished face, the slight flick of the hair and twitch of the shoulder, small fluctuations. The figure fastened his pace with new learned confidence. It was as he closed in on me that I knew. That familiar hook on his nose, the soft down on his cheek. My voice came out like a lost echo. It's you … Oliver … you are alive … you have been brought back … And then all had suddenly gone.

Chapter 11

On the morning of the penultimate day, both Anna and Teresa had been unable to sleep. Chance had been regaling all evening about his private club, di membri privati, describing with such earnest the characters he had come across, and Little Stan's drawn-out explanation of the importance of prefixes. And, they had drunk one too many cups of Stan's new coffee blend, the Geisha, which he had never tested on members of the public before, but as a way to thank Anna, he thought she might like its floral and tea-like quality.

Atypical of Teresa, she was also out of sorts and paced about the kitchen, feeling troubled. On the countertop, just behind the kettle, she noticed a displaced biscuit tin she didn't recognise. With little interest, just a pang of faint hunger, she opened it, hoping to find some custard creams. But what she found was a single letter. No envelope, just a page, hand-scripted. It was a letter of sorts, addressed to no one and very short. With a lot of full stops, presented a little like a poem with its vertical exposition. She read it multiple times, just to be sure she had understood what it was she was reading and what it all meant.

> I poisoned my mother.
> I placed it between two slices of bread.
> Sandwiched together.
> Lathered with jam.
> Stuffed with odourless death cap mushrooms.
> And water hemlock.
> Flavourless.
> Eight hours later she was dead.
> And then she was gone.

Chapter 12

Teresa and Anna sat at the kitchen table for their evening camomile tea and custard creams, talking about nothing in particular. Their thoughts perfectly aligned, needing no words. It was Teresa though that had come up with the idea of rearranging the breakfast table to create one celebratory feast where they would join their guests for their last breakfast. Big Stan would no doubt provide the beverages, Marybeth, the edible mushrooms (perhaps one of Monet's recipes with garlicky ceps), Little Stan plating all the non-yellow food, and Chance the vegan options. He would entertain everyone with ideas for his new book, *The Symbolism behind Gustave Moreau*, attributed to Oliver. Perhaps Teresa might even read one of Shakespeare's sonnets and Anna would most certainly recite from *The Little Girl Lost*. A true tryst had emerged.

No one had seemed the least bit surprised. They drank, ate, laughed and listened to one another. And when it was time for their eventual departures, Anna, never having been partial to over-elaborate farewells, simply waved as her first guests went on their merry ways. They heard Chance's final *addio* in the distance as they turned inside and Anna knew she no longer saw the paradox. As her guests drew their farewells, she espied the Colne River and the downy greenness as each perambulated along the non-aridity of the track that strengthened her resolve like a finally understood parable or the first understanding of the eponymous character. She also knew that in so many ways, it hadn't just been herself who had found emancipation, it had been all her guests that had realised their own freedoms. Little Stan, now impervious to ridicule; Chance, now self-assured; and Marybeth, whose liberty was once restricted by impediments was now released and she meditated over thoughts of Anna and Teresa as they read her confession which she had rehearsed over and over again, but now was out in the open, gratified and proud.

> *A returning image – he appeared once again amongst the carnage of the scene, flattened by what had happened. I heard the relentless noises of the sirens and screams, the metronome of wailing and I could see my mother inert behind the wheel and myself, lost behind her. Then, forever waiting for the silence to come and the noise dissipate, and this time it never returned.*

Anna and Teresa spent the afternoon on menial jobs, cleaning, polishing, dusting, undressing and dressing beds, shopping, and it was only when evening came that they sat beside each other and recovered the white satin guestbook and began to read … filled with promise.

Chapter 13

Then it was late spring in the year of 1966. The epitome of the decade, the year the Cup returned to Wembley, the year that Batman was first serialised on the television and the year full of colour and frivolous flamboyance.

So, exactly one year to the day, Anna and Teresa stood on their newly gravelled pathway to welcome the next five guests. Now with all the mustard-yellow of the rooms replaced in honour of Little Stan, and Anna who managed to track down two perfect reproductions of Gustave Moreau's most symbolic works: *The Apparition* (depicting Salome) and the watercolour, *Leda and the Swan* in homage to Chance's forthcoming literary success. For Marybeth, one of Nicholson's later paintings, simply titled *Mushrooms* as a paean to her stoic nature. And, finally for Teresa, who had never left Anna's side, she had chosen her favourite Shakespearean soliloquy, *Tomorrow, And Tomorrow, And Tomorrow* which replaced the pale green parrots on the stairwell, and together they buried the key to the lock on the upper floor. What Anna was most proud of though was finding an original edition of Robert Cawdrey's three-thousand-word dictionary dating back to the 1600s, which she placed next to the white satin guestbook.

The recently planted lilies were in full bloom, the scattering of delicate daisies, the yellow carnations and the papery roses bursting with flower. The Venetian ciabatta prepared for the grill and the cured meats ready for the table – all now worthy of her Italian descent, and all sorts of fresh goodies picked from their new garden, and the interiors now admirably furbished. No words needed to be spoken. Anna knew then that it is the stories that people choose to bring with them and the secrets they choose to tell that reveal most about them. And it was true to say that the memories of those first five guests were firmly engraved into the heart of *Lily*.

1966 was going to be a vintage year.

This book is printed on paper from sustainable sources managed under the Forest Stewardship Council (FSC) scheme.

It has been printed in the UK to reduce transportation miles and their impact upon the environment.

For every new title that Troubador publishes, we plant a tree to offset CO_2, partnering with the More Trees scheme.

For more about how Troubador offsets its environmental impact, see www.troubador.co.uk/sustainability-and-community